GW00393882

WITHDRAWN
LIBRARY

Reynard the Fox

Reynard the Fox

Based on the version by JOSEPH JACOBS

and retold by ROY BROWN

Illustrated by JOHN VERNON LORD

ABELARD-SCHUMAN

London · New York · Toronto

L.C.C.C. No. 69–14437
Standard Book No. 200 71602 6
PRINTED IN ENGLAND
by Cox & Wyman Limited
London, Fakenham and Reading

LONDON
Abelard-Schuman
Limited
8 King Street W.C.2

NEW YORK
Abelard-Schuman
Limited
6 West 57th Street

TORONTO
Abelard-Schuman
Canada Limited
1680 Midland Avenue

Contents

Foreword

These old stories have been told, in different forms and different languages, all over Europe, ever since the Middle Ages.

At first glance many of the tales seem heartless and cruel. The Fox, for instance, is not the sort of "hero" to look up to and try and imitate. He is a liar, a cheat and a coward, who uses every wicked and pitiless device imaginable to achieve his ends at the expense of everyone else. What is worse, he does not even get his just deserts at the end. His old rival and enemy, the Wolf, is little better: just as "red in tooth and claw", though less artful and more of an oaf. Even King Lion, who at first appears so noble, so full of fine sentiments, turns out, after all, to be weak, greedy and quite under the thumb (or paw!) of his vain and grasping wife.

It would have been easy, in retelling these stories, to have tacked on a "happy" ending; showing, say, the wretched victims having their own back and getting the better of their tormentors. But that is not how the stories were first told.

What must be remembered is that "Reynard the Fox" originated in a world very different, in some ways, from our own. Although the main characters are animals, they are really meant to represent people – types, rather than individuals. In the Middle Ages, over much of the world, ordinary folk were powerless, underprivileged and frequently ill-used by their rulers and their hirelings. Occasionally they had some redress, or they took matters into their own hands and wielded "pitchfork and stave" in the interests of justice. Then even the "Fox" sometimes came in for a sound thrashing. But all too often they were the prey of any adventurer and opportunist who could wheedle his way into the good graces of Authority.

However, there was some fun to be got out of the situation. Truly the story tellers (and, no doubt, their listeners) felt more than a grudging admiration for the Fox's cunning. Here and there the laughter *is* cruel. But there is no mockery of the innocents who suffered – unless it was considered that they had, to some extent, rather "asked for it." (Perhaps it is hard to feel complete sympathy for the really stupid!)

But beneath the fun and laughter there is a shudder. "Look out," the story spinners seem to be saying, at the end. "The Fox may have lost some of his coat, maybe his claws are a little blunted, but there he is, safely recovering in his lair, busily thinking up fresh outrages. If we don't unite against the evil he stands for, if we are too foolish to recognize true friends from false, real goodness from the mere pretence of good – then who knows? One day it may be *our* turn to be eaten!"

Whether our world, and the people in it, are so very different, or not, is something for the reader to think over. Although the tellers of folk-tales probably set out, first, to entertain, they had a great deal to teach; and they knew that in the behaviour of story characters we sometimes see, reflected, ourselves.

R.B.

1 Reynard is Accused

Each year in the spring the Lion, King of beasts, held a banquet at his palace in the forest. As all creatures were expected to attend, heralds were sent to all parts of the kingdom to summon them.

On this particular occasion, however, as soon as the animals assembled in front of the throne it was noticed that one was missing – Reynard the Fox. As usual he had mauled and robbed so many of his fellow creatures that the wily Fox thought it discreet to stay away from the spring celebrations. He knew very well that if he turned up he would be torn to pieces.

He was quite right. A long line of angry animals was waiting for a chance to complain of the Fox's behaviour. In fact, this part of the proceedings looked like taking all day. That was why Isegrim the Wolf pushed his way to the front with his entire family and, because he was one of the King's chief advisers, was allowed to speak first.

"Your Majesty, I beg of you to take pity on us. Not long ago the Fox broke into our home, subjected my family and myself to all sorts of insults, then spitefully blinded my poor children. When he was

told to appear before this court to answer charges, he merely made some scornful remark, scuttled off into a hole and hid. Since then he has committed every kind of wickedness, and I respectfully suggest, your Majesty, that it is high time he was punished as he richly deserves."

At the end of this speech a small dog managed to get to the front of the line and barked, "I also have a complaint, your Majesty. One bitter winter's day, I was lying on the bare earth freezing to death and half-starved, with nothing to eat but a little pudding. Suddenly, along came the Fox and snatched it from under my nose."

"Oh, that's an old story," sneered Tibert the Cat, leaping in front of the dog. "And besides, it was not *his* pudding. As a matter of fact, it belonged to me – I borrowed it from a miller while he was asleep."

The Panther snarled disagreeably at this. "The Cat is a fool. Does he suggest that the Fox should *not* be sent for and executed? Everyone knows that Reynard is a murderer, a thief and a vagabond, who loves only himself. Why, he would betray even the King of beasts for a chicken's leg! And only yesterday I saw the way he tormented Kyward the Hare. He had the poor little fellow between his knees and was pretending to teach him his prayers; then the wretch seized him by the throat and would have made an end of him had I not happened to be passing at the time."

"Hear, hear!" growled Isegrim the Wolf. "Let the Fox be hanged, then we shall all have peace."

"Oh, you hypocrite!" remarked Grimbard the Badger. He was Reynard's nephew, which is why he felt it proper to speak up on the Fox's behalf. "Do you pretend to be any kinder than my uncle? Well, you've done your share of biting in your time! What is more, everyone knows about the disgraceful way you robbed my uncle of a fish, leaving him only the dry bones; and what of the time you stole a piece of bacon, which Reynard had got with such difficulty that the farmer almost caught him in his sack? As for that mean little Hare, if he did not wish to be spanked he should have learned to say his prayers properly. My uncle was only acting as a good teacher should. Furthermore, are we to take any notice of the Dog's yappings? He as good as admitted that he stole the pudding from the Cat in the first place, and since when has it been a crime to steal from a thief? O King of beasts, let me tell the whole truth about my Uncle Reynard, before these spiteful creatures thoroughly blacken his name with their lies and exaggerations. Whatever he has done in the past, he has become a changed character. Now he has given up his home comforts and lives the humble life of a monk. He no longer hunts, refuses to eat meat, and trudges about in such a beggarly fashion that he has become as thin and pale as a shadow . . ."

The Badger had a great deal more to say of Reynard's spotless character, only at that moment there was a disturbance at the edge of the crowd and someone called out, "Make way for Chanticleer the Cock!"

They cleared a passage to the throne, and Chanticleer mournfully approached and bowed to the Lion. After the Cock came two young hens and a pair of pullets, all of them weeping bitterly, for between them they carried a bier on which lay the body of Chanticleer's daughter, Copple.

Then Chanticleer, beating his wings together in great sorrow, told his story.

2 Chanticleer the Cock's Story

Your Majesty (began the cock), let it be known that I once had eight brave sons and seven fair daughters, all of whom were hatched by my dear wife. We were, I may say, the most prized poultry in the land. So that we should be safe day and night from thieves and raiders we were allowed only to walk in a yard surrounded by a high stone wall. As six large fierce dogs were also appointed to keep watch over us, we naturally had nothing to fear.

But in time, Reynard the Fox grew jealous of the care that was taken of us and the comfort of our quarters, and did all he could to find a way, by some trickery or other, into our sanctuary. The dogs succeeded in scaring him off and sometimes he even got bitten for his trouble, but unfortunately he always managed to escape.

Then one day, the Fox turned up at the gate dressed as a monk. In one paw he carried a letter, properly sealed, which was supposed to proclaim a new royal law forbidding all creatures to fight or bear ill will towards one another.

The Fox's words seemed to have the ring of truth, and he added in the most humble tones, "Dear

Chanticleer, there is no longer any need to be afraid of me, for I have given up eating flesh of all kinds, and you have only to glance at me to see how thin and feeble I have grown. In fact, I have decided to spend the remainder of my days in fasting and good works. Excuse me if I hurry away, my friend, but I am already late for my evening prayers."

With that the Fox, muttering holy words, crept away and lay behind a hawthorn tree. Happy that now my children would be safe – or so I thought – I called them together for a walk outside the yard. No sooner had we strolled a few paces than the wicked Reynard slipped between us and the gate, snatched one of my children and put him into his knapsack, which he had hidden beneath his monk's cloak. Since then, O King of beasts, he has become so bold and greedy that even the dogs cannot keep him at bay. He has already eaten ten of my dear children and bitten off the head of the eleventh, my poor daughter Copple whom you see carried by her sorrowing sisters. Here is the sad proof that all I have told you about the traitorous and bloodthirsty Reynard is true.

There was a great moan of horror and indignation at Chanticleer's tale, and the King of beasts commanded that the dead pullet receive a decent burial at once. When the grave was dug, and the unfortunate bird lowered into it, a marble stone was set in place, upon which was inscribed:

COPPLE, CHANTICLEER'S DAUGHTER, WHOM
REYNARD THE FOX HATH SLAIN, LIETH
HERE BURIED. MOURN THOSE THAT
READETH IT, FOR HER DEATH WAS
UNJUST AND LAMENTABLE.

Then the Lion sent for his wisest advisers and a long discussion took place on how best to bring the crafty Fox to court for trial. In the end it was decided to send Bruin the Bear to fetch him. The Bear was a cheerful fellow who felt quite sure that however much the Fox's wiles fooled others, they would not trick *him*.

He set out jauntily towards Reynard's fortress, and everybody agreed that if he was still as lighthearted when he returned, then all would be well!

3 Bruin the Bear and the Honeycombs

In due course, Bruin the Bear arrived at Reynard's chief fortress which lay beyond a dark forest on the other side of a high mountain. The Bear found the gate locked and barred, so he sat on his tail and called out, "Hail, Cousin Fox! I bring a summons from his Majesty, King of beasts. You are to come with me to the palace, where you must answer those who accuse you of many wicked deeds. It is best that we go at once, or the king will be angry. Sir Reynard, can you hear me?"

Reynard the Fox had heard every word for he was crouched just on the other side of the fence where he had been sunning himself most pleasantly. But instead of answering the Bear, he darted into one of his tunnels to think out some way of avoiding this latest predicament.

Presently he came out of the hole, opened the gate and said, "My dear Bruin, do forgive my rudeness in not coming more quickly. As it happens I was saying my morning prayers. You are most welcome, but I wonder why King Lion sent an important person like you to fetch me to court? Why didn't he choose a more humble messenger, such as a sparrow? In

any case, I'm afraid our journey will be a slow one for I am not at all well today. It must be something I ate. You see, since I gave up meat I have had to swallow so many strange and unwholesome kinds of food."

"How dreadful!" said the Bear. "What exactly have you been eating?"

"Honeycombs! We poor foxes are not so high and mighty that we can pick and choose, you know. It was either honeycombs or starve."

"Honeycombs!" cried the Bear, for there is no delicacy more loved by his kind. "My dear Fox, you speak as though honeycombs were not fit to taste, yet surely you know there is no food more suitable for an emperor's feast. Just show *me* some honeycombs and I will be your devoted friend for ever."

The Fox chuckled. "Oh, you bears will have your little jokes!"

Bruin began to slobber with greed. "One does not make jokes about honeycombs, Fox. Are you trying to tell me that you actually know where some of this delicious food is to be found?"

"Enough for *ten* bears, and you will be very welcome to it. I hope I never have to taste it again! Look, not far away there lives a carpenter by the name of Lanfert. I happen to know that he has so much honey that it would take even a big fellow like you seven years to eat it. You may have every drop, and that shows how warm is my affection for you."

The Bear was pleased and flattered. How could he

guess that the wicked Fox was thinking: "What luck! Why, the stupid creature laughs and sings! Imagine what a different sort of tune he'll be humming soon!"

They set out at once for the carpenter's house. Only that morning, the man had dragged in a huge oak trunk from the forest, taken his axe and cut a great slit in it to enable the sun and air to dry out the inside. The slit was held wide open by means of two wedges, and the Fox chortled to himself when he pictured what would soon happen.

"There you are, Bruin," whispered Reynard as they crouched under some bushes. "In the oak trunk the honeycombs are packed so tightly that they are like peas in a pod." The Bear's eyes bulged. "But take care not to eat too much all at once. Honey is such rich food. I would never forgive myself if it made you ill!"

The Bear placed his feet firmly apart, leaned over the tree-trunk, then with a mighty thrust of his hairy body, drove his head into the slit. No sooner had it vanished into the tree than Reynard artfully removed the stout wedges. The slit snapped shut, like jaws, trapping the Bear, who kicked out his great hind legs and bellowed frantically.

"Enjoy your feast, dear Bruin," cried Reynard from the bushes. "If the honey sticks in your throat, beg the farmer to bring you a drink of water to wash it down. Whatever you do, don't gobble *all* the honey or it will make you too fat to run back to the palace!"

Then the Fox, well-pleased with his morning's

work, slunk off to his fortress. Meanwhile the carpenter heard the pitiful bellowings and ran from his house. Seeing the Bear stuck in the tree, ears and all, he called upon his neighbours to help him. Eventually the entire town was aroused, and people came along armed with any weapons they could lay their hands on: goads, rakes, brooms – and, making a ring round the poor trapped Bear, they beat him until he was half dead.

Bruin the Bear bellowed louder still, terrified and in agony. When he got loose, at last, it was only at the cost of much skin and both ears, which he left behind in the tree-trunk together with the fur from his front paws. At last he managed to reach the river. One of his pursuers struck him such a blow on the head that he was stunned and blinded. He lashed out in all directions, and that was how he accidentally knocked the priest's wife into the river. She couldn't swim, so the people had to rescue her instead of paying attention to the Bear. Bruin escaped by swimming to the far bank where, in utter misery, he threw himself down.

Even then his ordeal was not over. Reynard, thinking himself now safe, had been cheerfully catching chickens. He was on his way home, singing, when he saw Bruin lying on the river bank. "That fool of a carpenter!" he muttered to himself. "To think that he had such a fine lump of bear-meat under his very nose, and he let it escape."

The Bear saw him and moaned, "Oh, red villain, what have you done to me?"

The Fox sounded most indignant. "What are you grumbling about? It was *you* that stole the honeycombs and I don't suppose you paid a penny piece for them! And what on earth are you lying there for, with your ears cropped and half your skin missing from your head and paws? Have you mislaid your cap and gloves?"

Then, with many more taunts the Fox went singing on his way. As for the Bear, finding it far too painful to walk, he proceeded to roll head over heels all the way back to the palace, pushing himself along with his tail.

The King of beasts was furious when he heard what had happened. He called his advisers to decide what should be done next, and that was how Tibert the Cat came to be chosen as the second messenger.

4 The Cat and the Priest's Barn

King Lion admired Tibert the Cat's wise and serious character. So he sent for him and said, "Your job is to bring the Fox here so that we can deal with him. He is always polite to you. Point out to him that if he gets up to any more of his tricks, he will wish he had never been born."

Tibert the Cat did not want to go on this errand at all. "O King of beasts, send someone stronger and bolder. We cats are not like bears or wolves."

"I chose you because you are wise," said King Lion, "and sometimes cunning succeeds where force fails. Now off you go."

The Cat obeyed, but as he got ready for the journey he was thinking: "I only hope my luck holds, but I feel sure everything will go wrong."

With such gloomy thoughts he set out for the forest. On his way he met a bird, and called out, "Bird, please turn and fly on my right side."

The Cat, who believed in magic and fortune-telling, watched the bird to see what it would do. If it obeyed his instructions, all would be well. But unfortunately it turned and flew in the opposite direction and this made Tibert utterly miserable.

At length he reached the fortress over the mountain and cried, "Sir Reynard! The King of beasts bids you to attend his court. If you refuse to accompany me, it will be the worse for you."

Reynard appeared at once, full of welcoming smiles. "Greetings dear Tibert, and health to the King of beasts. Of course I will obey his commands – tomorrow! Tonight, come and stay with me. Then at sunrise we will make the journey together."

The last thing the Cat wanted was to sleep in the same room as the Fox. Trembling he said, "But there is a full moon tonight, so let us go at once."

"The night is full of perils," replied Reynard. "Besides, you must be hungry after your long walk.

Come and share what little I have. Honeycombs, perhaps?"

Reluctantly the Cat went in. He turned up his nose at honeycombs. "They might be all right for bees and bears, no doubt. Personally I prefer mice."

"Mice?" chuckled the Fox. "My dear Tibert, this must be your lucky day. I know where there are so many mice that if they were to scuttle under the eaves of a house the roof would fall in under their weight."

The Cat forgot his fright! "Show me, Sir Reynard, and you will win a friend for life."

So the Fox explained that the mice were to be found in a barn which belonged to a priest who lived near by. Tibert, panting with greed and excitement, ran after Reynard and soon they reached the priest's barn. It was built of stout mud walls. Only the night before, the Fox had burrowed a hole clean through into the barn and stolen one of the priest's fat chickens. Reynard knew very well that the priest had set a gin trap on the other side of the wall in order to catch him the moment he squeezed through a second time.

He told Tibert, "Listen to the mice squeaking. They are simply begging to be eaten!" The Cat listened, and thought that he could hear the squeaks, although it was really only the wind in the eaves. "A creature as delightfully slim as you may easily slip through the hole. Waste no time, my friend. I will await your return and when you have finished your feast we'll set off at once for the palace."

The Cat hesitated, trying to look through the hole. "Those priests are crafty fellows," he grumbled. "Do you think it will be safe?"

"Are you afraid of shadows?" mocked Reynard. And since no cat likes to be thought a coward, Tibert shut his eyes, poked his head into the opening, and his neck was promptly caught in the trap. The more he tugged the tighter the snare grasped him.

Reynard the Fox found all this most amusing. "How do the mice taste, friend Tibert?" he jeered.

"I hope they will not give you indigestion. Why not ask the priest to bring you sauce to improve their taste? Ah, if only Isegrim the Wolf were here to share the banquet with you!"

Then the Fox slipped happily away in the dark. The Cat made such a noise with his screams and curses that the entire household next door was awakened. The priest tumbled out of bed, crying, "We have caught the Fox that stole the hen! Let us go and get rid of him."

He gathered his wife and servants together, then they lit candles, picked up handy weapons, hastened to the barn and flayed the Cat until he had lost one eye and most of his fur. Only by scratching and biting his tormentors was he able to escape. Then, unable to place his sore feet upon the ground, the unhappy creature tumbled in a ball back to the palace, where King Lion once again angrily summoned his advisers.

5 How Reynard Confessed to Grimbard the Badger

Most of the animals wanted King Lion to send an army to Reynard's fortress and put an end to him. But his nephew, Grimbard the Badger, said, "However wicked he may have been, by law a creature of such noble rank must be sent for three times. Then if he refuses to come, send the army."

"But who will risk his ears, and his life, in fetching him?" asked the King of beasts.

"I will," offered the Badger.

"Then take care," warned King Lion. "Just because the Fox is your uncle, that doesn't mean he won't treat you as disgracefully as he has everyone else."

In due course, Grimbard the Badger arrived at Reynard's gate. "Welcome, Nephew," said the Fox. "Of course I will come with you. But let it be understood that I have no intention of arguing with that rabble at court who have accused me so unfairly. I will go for the simple reason that the kingdom cannot be properly governed without my help. Why did I leave the court in the first place? I will tell you. It was because I was tired of the gossip and the spiteful tales that were told about me. However, I am ready to forgive them all – even the King himself, though in my opinion he should know better than to believe every chatterbox who whispers in his ear."

So Reynard the Fox said goodbye to his wife and children, who shed many tears for him. Then the two animals set off for the palace. On the way the Fox pretended to grow solemn and heavy-hearted. "Oh, alas!" he sighed, putting on a hang-dog look. "How wicked I have been!"

Then he begged the Badger to hear his confessions, for, he said, everyone knew how good and pure

Grimbard was. The Badger, who did not in the least mind being thought so good, willingly offered to listen. So Reynard, with many sighs, confessed how he had been the cause of Tibert the Cat having his neck caught in the gin trap at the priest's barn; how he had often eaten the Chanticleer's innocent chicks, disobeyed the King of beasts and pretended to become a monk just to make it easier to catch small animals and put them in his knapsack. There was also the time when he had fastened his old enemy, Isegrim the Wolf, to a bell-rope, and when the bell rang the villagers had flocked to the scene with sticks and almost beat the Wolf to death.

"Not long afterwards," went on the Fox, "I taught him to catch fish, and he got a good beating for that, too! Then I led him to a priest's house where, as I happened to know, there was a delicious piece of bacon. The Wolf ate so much that he grew too fat to squeeze through the door and make his escape. I howled until the townsfolk arrived with pitchforks and thrashed him to within an inch of his life. While all that was happening I slipped into the next room where the priest was at dinner, stole a roast chicken, and was turning my back when the man threw a knife at me and cried, "Kill the Fox!" A huge crowd pursued me, so I led them to Isegrim's hiding-place, dropped the chicken, and escaped through a hole, leaving the Wolf to take the blame. You should have seen the punishment they gave that poor fellow, beating him with sticks and stones and clubs until he was half-dead!

"And have I ever mentioned that business of the Cock and seven hens? Well, I once led Isegrim to a heavy door behind which, I told the Wolf, perched a Cock and seven hens all in a row. The fool poked his head through the door and said, 'I can see nothing – it is so dark.' 'Look harder,' I said. Then I gave him a gentle push, and he fell headlong into a pit. He made such a noise when he landed at the bottom that the householders awoke at once, grabbed their candles and weapons and Isegrim carries the scars of that thrashing to this very day. Oh, alas, alas, good Badger, how can I ever be forgiven for these terrible crimes?"

The Badger solemnly thought it over, then he said, "By leading a kind and gentle life from now on, Uncle. You must do good works, give alms to beggars and say your prayers three times a day."

"I will begin at once," promised the Fox, and they walked on until presently they met a flock of geese, ducks and hens who were strolling peacefully along. Reynard promply seized a plump pullet in his mouth and if it hadn't been nimble-witted enough to flap its wings and screech, it would have been gobbled up on the spot.

"Shame, Uncle, shame!" cried the Badger. "How weak of you to give way to temptation so easily."

"True, Nephew," said the Fox. "My eye wandered!"

After this Reynard stared greedily at every innocent fowl in sight until Grimbard the Badger clicked his tongue disgustedly and asked, "Uncle Reynard, why do you look so hungrily at those chickens?"

"Oh, I was not thinking of *eating* them," protested the Fox. "I was offering up prayers for their future happiness and health."

"Really?" sighed the Badger, doubtfully. "For a Fox saying his prayers you have such a strange look on your face!"

However, the Fox behaved himself quite well for the rest of the journey, and at last they reached the palace in the forest.

6 How Reynard Answered his Accusers

When the news spread that the Fox and Grimbard the Badger had arrived, a great host of animals hurried to the palace. The mere sight of the crowd, all howling and shrieking for his blood, made Reynard turn pale. Nevertheless, he put on a bold front and strutted to the throne with all the dignity and hauteur of a prince.

"Noble and merciful King of beasts," he said. "It is well known that I have always been one of your Majesty's most loyal and devoted subjects. How thankful I am that you never listen to court gossip, or pay attention to tale-tellers."

"Silence!" roared King Lion. "And don't expect us to sit here listening to you just because of your smooth, sly tongue. Look around you at these unfortunate creatures whom you have wronged, and understand that you are about to pay for your crimes with your worthless life."

Reynard the Fox quaked, then glanced at Bruin the Bear who sat in the most important place beside the King of beasts. "I suppose the Bear has accused me of some injury he has suffered? A likely tale! Was it my fault that when you sent him to summon me to court, he wasted his time stealing the carpenter's honey and got a sound beating and lost his ears for his impudence? As for Tibert the Cat, he has only himself to blame for losing an eye through poking his nose into a mouse's nest."

But these excuses only made things worse for the Fox. With howls and screams the Ram, the Bear, the Cat, the Wolf, the Panther, the Boar, the Camel, the Goose, the Kid, the Colt, the Ass, the Bull, the Ox, the Weasel and Chanticleer the Cock all denounced him so ferociously that the King of beasts had no alternative but to arrest him on the spot and order that he be hanged at once.

Tibert the Cat said, "Let us get it over with quickly. Look, the sun is setting and once it begins to get dark, that rogue will try to slip off into the forest."

"But where are the gallows?" asked Isegrim the Wolf. "We can't hang him without gallows."

"Who cares about gallows?" sighed the Fox, overhearing this. "Oh, make use of the rope that Tibert still has round his neck – the one the miller tried to choke him with when he stole that pudding! And let the Cat be my executioner if he fancies the job. Be sure I don't escape!"

The Wolf tittered. "That's the best advice you've ever given us, Fox. Away with him!"

Then they bundled the Fox off to a place of execution, where the King and Queen and a great crowd of onlookers gathered to watch.

"Cat, climb up with the rope," ordered Isegrim the Wolf. "Bear, mind this fellow doesn't escape while I hold the ladder."

"Wait!" cried Reynard the Fox. "Before I die, I wish to confess my crimes so that my soul may be at peace. Surely I may be granted such a small mercy?"

The court could scarcely refuse this request, so the Fox was allowed to speak. All the same, Bruin the Bear kept a sharp eye on him in case this was just another one of his tricks.

"When I was a young fox cub," began Reynard, "I was as innocent as any of you. Then one day, as I was playing with some young lambs, I accidentally bit one. Tasting sheep's blood for the first time had a strange effect on me. After that, I just could not stop myself from catching goats, sheep and wild fowl, and I must admit that sometimes I ate them with enjoyment. But my greatest downfall came when I met the Wolf, this same Isegrim who is now so close to the ear of the King. He told me that he was my uncle, and that if I copied everything he did I would eventually grow as strong and wise as he.

"He was quite right, of course. It was not long before I became just as ferocious and merciless, for I was quick to learn. We went everywhere together and, at first, he stole the big animals and I only the small ones. Naturally, he took the biggest share of everything, and to tell the truth he tore his victims to pieces with such savagery that I was fortunate if I got as much as a ram's bone or a calf's hoof.

"I soon realized that if I remained the Wolf's partner I would never grow rich. Luckily, I had no need of wealth because by that time I owned a hoard of treasure great enough to fill twenty carts, but that is another story. It would be best not to tell it, since it relates to a wicked plot to kill the King of beasts and steal his crown."

There was great excitement when the Fox mentioned this, and King Lion immediately demanded to hear the entire story. But Reynard the Fox sighed deeply and tears sprang to his eyes as he said, "Your Majesties, I would rather die than disclose what happened. Not only members of my own family, alas, but many who stand beside you in high positions are characters in the play which is all true, about stolen treasure. But I beg you not to force me to name the traitors concerned, but rather get on at once with the business of hanging me."

Now, the King of beasts did not believe a word of the Fox's strange story, but the Queen insisted upon hearing the rest, and as she usually got her own way Reynard was told to speak.

This is the tale he told . . .

7 The Treasure at Crekenpit

Long ago (began Reynard the Fox) my father happened to dig a hole, and at the bottom of it he found a great treasure which, it turned out, had belonged to a famous king of another country. At first, my father was merely curious to learn how such precious things had got there, but after he had let the glittering collection trickle through his paws for a while, and watched the sun's rays sparkle on it, he allowed his discovery to go completely to his head. From that day he no longer thought of himself as a humble fox but as a kind of emperor.

He immediately sent for Tibert the Cat who was told to bring Bruin the Bear, and later they were joined by my nephew, Grimbard the Badger and Isegrim the Wolf. Together they hatched a plot to overthrow our King and set the crown on the Bear's head.

Unluckily the Badger got drunk and told his wife the whole story. She told my wife, who promised never to let on, but like all women she couldn't keep a secret and told me about it.

I was heavy-hearted to learn that my own father was a traitor. Also, I knew very well that if the Bear were made King, our beautiful land would no longer be fit to live in, for we all know what a brutal and greedy race the bears are.

I realized that your Majesty's life was in my hands, so I made up my mind to find this treasure myself. I kept watch on my father, knowing that every night he crept off to the hiding-place to gloat over his hoard like a miser. I did not have to wait long. One night I saw him emerge from a secret hole which he afterwards stuffed with sand. Then he licked over his own footprints to smooth them and patted the area with his tail, so that it would have been impossible for a casual passer-by to see where my father had been. How cunning, I thought!

As soon as he had gone, I scraped away the sand and found myself in a cave, and there lay the priceless treasure. I fetched my wife and between us we managed to carry it off to a new hiding-place. Then we sat back and waited to see what would happen.

Now, the traitors were making their final plans for seizing the throne. They had enlisted a host of soldiers from other countries until over a thousand rebels were gathered under the Bear's banner. Of course, all these fellows had to be paid, and then there was the cost of their arms and ammunition, so you can imagine how put out my father and his henchmen were when they went to the cave and found the treasure gone. In fact, my father was so heart-broken that he went straight to the nearest tree and hanged himself. The rest of the traitors simply scattered, pretending that the whole affair had never taken place. What happened to them afterwards, and to what high positions they have climbed, we can see for ourselves simply by looking around! Is anyone here surprised that I have been slandered to the point of being executed, despite all my loyalty to the King and Queen of beasts?

And with this fine speech, and many tears to go with it, Reynard the Fox wrung his paws so pitifully that Queen Lion insisted that he be released at once. Then she and the King took the Fox aside and asked him privately where the treasure was hidden. After

all, this was the chief reason why they had set him free!

"It is hidden by the river at a place called Crekenpit," said Reynard. "The river runs through a desert where hardly any creature goes. There are two birch trees growing on the bank, and the hoard lies directly under the roots of the second one."

King Lion was still less inclined to believe in the story than his Queen. But as she pointed out, "If it were a pack of lies, would the Fox have made his own father the chief actor in such a despicable affair?"

The King thought Reynard *was* quite capable of doing such a thing, but, at last, he reluctantly promised to pardon the Fox. There were two conditions: one, that Reynard should promise never again to hunt or harm his fellow creatures and, two, that he should lead King Lion to the hidden treasure without delay.

"I wish it were possible, your Majesty," sighed the Fox. "The fact is that I have been given such a bad reputation by my enemies that I must go to Rome and obtain the Pope's pardon. After that, I shall travel to the Holy Land, and not return until I have made my peace with the whole world. But Kyward the Hare knows where Crekenpit is, and he will gladly show you the way."

The King of beasts could not set himself up against such an important person as the Pope, so there was nothing to be done but to allow Reynard to make his pilgrimage. King Lion, therefore, mounted his throne and announced, "Listen all of you. Let it be known that Reynard the Fox is one of the chief servants of our household. Whatever wrongs he may have done in the past are hereby pardoned. Take care to treat him with proper respect and kindness, and let me hear no more tales about his alleged crimes or it will be the worse for you!"

And the King and Queen of beasts invited Reynard the Fox to stand with them by the throne, and all the creatures applauded to show that they were loyal subjects and bore the Fox no ill will.

8 How Reynard Again Deceived the King

Guessing how matters were likely to turn out, the Wolf, the Bear and the Cat had already hidden themselves. However, the Raven found them and said, "Reynard the Fox is now in the King's good graces. He has told all kinds of lies about you, and as a result you are about to become slaves."

Bruin and Isegrim hurried to King Lion to defend themselves, but Tibert the Cat, frightened out of his wits, slunk even farther away. The first two were immediately placed under arrest and Reynard inwardly chortled with delight. Making the best of his new-won favour with the Queen, he begged for some of the Bear's skin out of which to make a new knapsack. He also wanted the skin off the wolf's paws to provide him with thick shoes to protect his own feet from the sharp stones on the way to the Holy Land. "While you are about it," he added, "I will have the She-wolf's paw-skins for a spare pair of shoes."

"Certainly, dear Reynard," agreed the Queen, who could scarcely wait to set her hands on the treasure. "After all their spitefulness they deserve to suffer a little pain."

The operations were carried out, and as the poor

She-wolf writhed in agony the Fox mocked her. "Take comfort, dear Aunt. Since I shall wear your paws to Rome, the Pope will, in a way, be giving *you* his blessing!"

So the next day Reynard got ready for his pilgrimage, putting on the new shoes taken from the Wolf, slinging the bear-skin knapsack on his back, and wearing his monk's habit. Then he said to Bellin the Ram and Kyward the Hare, "You two fine fellows are the kindest and gentlest of creatures, much as I was myself when I first became a monk. Come, my pair of amiable grass-eaters, and we will walk to Rome together."

The unfortunate Ram and Hare dared not refuse this invitation, and in any case Reynard the Fox looked perfectly innocent in his monk's cowl.

First they called at the Fox's fortress to bid farewell to his wife and children. At the gate, Reynard said to Bellin the Ram, "Wait here, my friend. You will find plenty of sweet grass to eat. Kyward and I will go indoors where we have certain private matters to talk over."

The Fox's wife was overjoyed to see that her breadwinner had come home. "It was not easy to make my peace with the King and Queen of beasts," sighed the Fox. "In the end, however, they realized that I was innocent, and were so sorry that they sent us a gift to make amends."

"Oh, where is the gift?" cried the She-fox.

"Here beside me!" smiled the Fox, and he

promptly slew poor Kyward the Hare whom they made into a tasty stew. They enjoyed their feast so much that they forgot all about Bellin the Ram until he began stamping on the ground and calling, "Hurry, Reynard my friend. We must begin our journey."

"Patience!" called Reynard, but soon he appeared at the gate. The bear-skin knapsack bulged strangely!

"I thought I heard Kyward the Hare call out for help a while ago," said the Ram.

"No, no!" said Reynard. "When she heard that I am to go all the way to Rome and then to the Holy Land, my poor wife fainted with the shock. Kyward thought she was dead – that is why he squealed. Now he is comforting her, for she has always behaved like an affectionate aunt towards him. Good Bellin, why don't you go on ahead? I have a most important errand for you. Here are some secret letters to the King of beasts. Kyward will catch up with you presently."

"Oh, very well," said Bellin the Ram, and he took the knapsack and placed it on his back.

"Whatever you do," said Reynard the Fox, "do not peep inside. The letters are *most* secret, and so important that King Lion is sure to reward you handsomely for their safe delivery."

Bellin the Ram was pleased with this prospect, so without argument he set out on the road back to the palace. When he arrived, he was taken to the King of beasts and the knapsack was handed over.

"Secret letters!" muttered the King, very intrigued. He sent for his secretary, who could read all sorts of languages, then Tibert the Cat helped his Majesty to open the knapsack.

Out fell not letters – but the Hare's head!

"Woe is me that I ever listened to that wretched murderer, the Fox!" wailed the King. "And to think that the Bear, the Wolf and the She-wolf all lost some of their skin to provide him with comforts."

"Most unfortunate," agreed the Leopard. "But at least there is a way to make it up to them. Of course the Fox is not here, so at present we cannot punish

him. However, in my humble opinion the Ram is to blame for letting himself be tricked, so let *him* suffer the consequences. Later we can gather an army and destroy the wicked Reynard in his fortress."

This all seemed fair and sensible, so King Lion sent the Leopard to the prison where the unfortunate Bruin and Isegrim lay chained to the wall. "The King has pardoned you," announced the Leopard. "According to a new law he has just made, you and your descendants may freely prey upon the Ram and his family for ever. You also have royal permission to hunt down and kill all foxes – if and when you can find them."

So the Bear and the Wolf were set free, and to celebrate the new law a great feast was held. Practically every animal of note was present and everybody had a splendid time.

But in the midst of the music and dancing, Coney the Rabbit scuttled to the throne and begged the King of beasts to listen to a fresh complaint. "Your Majesty, I happened to be passing Reynard's fortress yesterday when whom should I meet but the Fox himself, dressed as a simple pilgrim. I greeted him in a friendly way, thinking he must have become good and kind, but he attacked me most savagely and I was lucky to escape with my life. As it is, he nearly knocked my head off with a cruel sweep of his paw and, as you can see I lost one of my ears."

The Rabbit had scarcely finished his tale when the Rook flew to the throne and said miserably,

"This very day my wife and I were strolling peaceably on the heath when, to our astonishment, we came across the Fox lying on his back. He was panting so pitifully that we thought he was drawing his last breath. We ventured near, and my wife, who was a kind and sympathetic bird, placed her head in the Fox's mouth in order to listen for signs of life. What did the wretch do but snap his jaws shut, biting off her head, and if I hadn't flown to the highest branch of a tree I, too, would have been eaten alive. Here, your Majesty, is all that is left of my dear wife – a few tattered feathers!"

The Rook laid these at the King's feet with much sorrow, and for some time his Majesty was beside himself with fury, his roars shaking the ground.

Of course the Wolf and the Bear were happy with the way matters had turned out, but the Queen of beasts was still inclined to be on the Fox's side. "It is all very well," she said, "but how do we know that the Rabbit didn't deserve to lose an ear? Suppose it was the She-rook's own fault that her head got bitten off? In any case, in my opinion it would be quite wrong to hunt the Fox down with weapons and armies. As a King's adviser he deserves to be summoned to court in the proper way, then tried according to law."

With this the Leopard, who was an expert in legal matters, agreed whole-heartedly – much to the annoyance of Isegrim the Wolf, who pointed out, "If the Fox had any excuses to offer for his behaviour he would have come here himself to explain, not wait to be dragged to court in disgrace. And what about the treasure of Crekenpit? Isn't it perfectly clear by now that he managed to put over another of his wiles for eluding justice? Are we to let him go around pretending to be a holy monk so that he can more easily prey on innocent birds and small animals? Not that I am presuming to criticize your Majesties, who, in their wisdom, allowed the wretch to go scot free!"

The hint was not lost on King Lion, who shuffled uncomfortably and said, "If the Fox does not appear to answer these new charges, we will go and fetch him, armed with pikestaffs, bows, arrows, guns and swords."

9 The Wolf and the Mare's Colt

Grimbard the Badger was distressed to think what might happen to his wayward uncle, so he hurried away in secret to warn him.

He discovered Reynard in the forest dealing in his customary fashion with two young pigeons which, while learning to fly, had unhappily fallen from their tree straight into the waiting fox's claws.

When the Badger described what had occurred at court, Reynard merely said, "Cheer up, Nephew! You heard a few fine speeches full of fire and woe. You saw a sprinkling of tears shed on the grass. But just wait till we get to the palace and I cast my spell on those dolts! Why, in the end, we'll have them all clapping and cheering. Besides, the King of beasts knows very well that without me to help govern the kingdom he might as well give it away to the sparrows. Come, Nephew, let me hear you laugh. Join me in tasting these fine pigeons, then after supper we will start upon our journey."

It was while they travelled together that Reynard the Fox told the tale of the Wolf and the Mare's colt.

It happened that not long ago I met Isegrim the

Wolf in a wood (began the Fox). Not far away stood a fine grey mare with a plump, healthy colt by her side. At this time Isegrim was half-dead with hunger, so he said to me, "My good Reynard, do me a service. Go and ask that mare if she will sell me her colt."

"Certainly," said I, "for it makes me sad to see you so hungry, Wolf. Wait here and I will see what I can do. The Mare will listen to me."

I walked to the Mare and inquired, "Madam, what will you take for your fine colt?"

"Money," said she, for all horses have witty tongues.

"But how much?"

"The exact price is written on my left rear hoof. Come and read it for yourself."

"Well," I said, "as it happens I am no great scholar, and in any case I am not the one who requires the colt, but my friend the Wolf who lies sick and hungry across the field."

"Then let him make his own deal," said the Mare.

So I went back to Isegrim and told him, "You shall soon have your supper. All you have to do is read the price of the colt, which is written on the Mare's left rear hoof. The colt is sure to be cheap."

Now, as everyone knows, the Wolf is among the vainest of all creatures, and when I asked Isegrim if he could read he bellowed in the most unseemly fashion, saying, "Read, Fox? Why, I have a great knowledge not only of English but of Latin, Greek, French and Dutch. It will be easy to discover the price of the colt."

Then he forgot his sickness and hunger and loped across to the spot where the Mare was waiting. I watched what happened from a suitable refuge under the bushes.

I presume the Wolf asked the price of the colt, for the Mare raised her left rear hoof and Isegrim bent his head to peer at it, trying to read what he imagined was written there. His nose was close to the iron shoe when the Mare lunged out, landing poor Isegrim such a blow that he turned several somersaults, picked himself up and scampered shakily towards me.

"Poor Isegrim," I greeted him. "What has happened? Have you eaten so much young horse-meat that it has given you indigestion? And what precisely was written upon the Mare's hoof? Was it in prose or verse? Perhaps it was a jolly song you read, for I swear I saw you sing and dance. I had no idea that you were expert in so many arts!"

"Even if you had a heart of stone you would pity me more," howled the silly fellow. "How was I to know that the letters I saw were really shoe-nails?"

"The trouble with you, Cousin, is that you have strained your eyes with too much study!" And so I taunted him until he grew bad-tempered and showed his teeth. You can always be certain, dear Grimbard, that when he meets with some small difficulty the Wolf will turn vicious and disagreeable.

"Do you think I behaved wickedly, Nephew?" asked Reynard, when he had finished his story.

"Yes," said the Badger, who then proceeded to offer all kinds of good advice for the saving of his uncle's black soul. But by this time, since they were drawing near the King of beasts' palace, Reynard was beginning to tremble again, so he did not listen very intently to what Grimbard said.

10 The She-ape Speaks up for Reynard

Once more a great crowd was gathered at the King's throne and, putting on his most innocent air, Reynard opened his mouth to offer his excuses. King Lion, however, was in no mood to listen to fresh deceit. "Hold your tongue!" he roared. "We have no use for your honeyed words today. If we allow you to speak at all, it is only because you have such a short time to live. You have shown how honourably you keep your promises by the way you have treated the unfortunate Rabbit and the Rook's wife."

At this Reynard howled pitifully. "Oh, what have I done this time? What lies have been told by those I thought were my dear friends? I will tell you the truth of what happened to the Rabbit. When he arrived at my house I gave him some meat because he was hungry. I had no use for it, because since I became a monk I never eat meat on Fridays. Now, it happened that one of my little cubs thought the Rabbit was robbing us, so he lost his temper and bit off his ear. Surely nobody is going to blame an innocent fox cub for trying to defend his family?

"As for the Rook, he came to me full of cawings and croakings because he had just lost his wife.

Naturally, I said how sorry I was at his news and tried to comfort him. Instead of being grateful, the wretched bird apparently flew here and accused me of eating his wife. How does he think I caught her? Am I supposed to have grown wings overnight? And if your Majesty is wondering why I am not on my way to Rome, that is simply because I happened to meet my uncle the Ape. He is a great friend of the Pope, you know. He said he would obtain his holiness's pardon for me and save an unnecessary journey."

"What about the Hare's head Bellin the Ram brought me in the knapsack?" demanded the King of beasts.

"Oh, *that*!" gasped Reynard the Fox, and being stuck for words all of a sudden, he tried a fainting fit, and the creatures beside him had to prop him up. It would have been most unfortunate had not his aunt, the She-ape, decided it was time she put in a helpful word out of family loyalty.

"Your Majesty," she said. "I think everyone here will agree that I have a right to speak on the Fox's behalf, since he is obviously too ill to defend himself. After all, I have always been respected as one who knows the law of the land. For instance, when I made a pilgrimage to Rome, the Pope provided me with a bed of straw, whereas the other animals had to make do with the stone floor. That was how much his Holiness valued my advice. Now it is my duty to remind your Majesty that the Foxes have, for many generations, given better service to the court than either the Wolves or the Bears. When have *their* opinions about anything been worth a penny?"

"That's all very well," grumbled the King. "But it was not your head that was sent to me in a knapsack! If you want to praise this fellow, that is up to you. As far as I can remember, the Fox has never performed any deed that has not led to some poor, weak creature's downfall."

"Tut, tut!" said the She-ape. "Can your Majesty have forgotten the business of the Snake and the hedge?"

Clearly the King of beasts *had* forgotten, so the She-ape told the story again.

It was about two years ago (began the She-ape) when a man visited this court carrying a Snake by the throat. It appeared that the Snake had been in the act of crawling through a hedge and got its head caught in a trap. The man had happened to come along, and naturally the Snake had begged him to release it.

"All right," said the man, "but you must promise not to bite me afterwards."

The Snake gave its promise, the man set it free, and for a mile or two they walked along together. Everything was going well, the pair behaving like the best of friends, until suddenly the Snake turned and bit the man on the leg.

"Ouch! Why did you bite me?" demanded the

man. "Didn't you promise not to harm me if I freed you from the trap?"

"Yes, that is perfectly true," agreed the Snake. "But I am hungry and that makes a difference. It is the law of the land that any creature may kill for food."

"I don't believe it," said the man, who was very annoyed. "Wait until we meet another judge of the matter and listen to what he has to say."

As it happened the first creature they met was the Raven, who offered the opinion that the man should be eaten. Mind you, he didn't say this because he cared much for the law – he was only hoping for a share of the feast!

The man said, "The Raven is a thief. Are we to listen to the opinion of a thief?"

So they went on until they met the Bear and the Wolf. This pair, as might be expected, advised the Snake to eat the man at once. The Snake darted at the man with its poisonous tongue, but he jumped aside just in time, crying out, "You do me wrong!"

"How so?" asked the Snake in surprise. "We have now had the opinions of three creatures, all of whom agreed that I should eat you."

"The Bear and the Wolf are riff-raff and murderers," complained the man. "We shouldn't take notice of what they say. Lead me to your King at once, for I will listen only to his opinion."

So the man was brought along to the palace, and that was when you, King of beasts, begged Reynard the Fox to give his counsel. The Fox said, "Let us put the Snake back in the hedge and see how he looked in the trap."

This was done at once, and as soon as the Snake was secured, my Nephew said, "Now, if the man thinks the Snake will eat him after it is freed, he had better go away and leave it to its fate."

This, of course, is just what the man did, and as far as I know the Snake is still there, which serves it right! The point is, I remember how we all applauded the Fox for his wise counsel.

11 The Wonderful Gems

This story made a good impression and a great many of the animals had second thoughts about executing the Fox. However, to make the best of the situation the She-ape now called her entire family to stand beside Reynard as a sign that he was not friendless and unbeloved.

"King of beasts, see how many champions the Fox has," cried the She-ape. "I beg you to let Reynard again speak on his own behalf. Of course, if it turns out that he is guilty we will not stand in the way of his proper punishment."

Much emboldened, Reynard the Fox took a deep breath and said, "Let me tell you how grieved I was to hear that my little friend Kyward the Hare is dead! And what, I beg you, has become of Bellin the Ram? Why, only yesterday I gave him a most important parcel to bring to your Majesties. In fact, there were three small bundles, two of which were for the Queen of beasts, and they all contained wonderful gems."

"Gems?" gasped the Queen, pricking up her ears.

"What gems?" roared the King. "All I received was a knapsack containing the Hare's head. The

Ram said you had given him the knapsack, and I had him punished for his part in the affair. I saw no other bundles."

"Oh, alas!" sighed Reynard. "There go the three most extraordinary gems that ever belonged to a prince. And to think that I went to all the trouble of digging them out of the ground at Crekenpit. I would rather die than be told that your Majesties had been deceived and robbed of so much!"

"Never mind," said the She-ape, anxious that her nephew should not spoil his story with too much embroidery. "We can easily appoint a magician to find them."

"Such wonderful gems. The like of these the world will never see again," went on the Fox. "Woe, woe, woe . . ." And with many such sounds of misery, he told the court why the gems were of such great worth.

The first gem (said Reynard) is a ring of the finest gold. It is inscribed with letters of a nature I cannot read, but a friendly magician whom I met on the road one day told me that whoever wears this ring will for ever be free of the evils of witchcraft; neither will thunder or lightning be able to harm him. Also he will at no time be too hot or too cold.

The setting of the ring contains three different stones. The first, which is red, glows like burning coals so that when the wearer walks at night his path is brightened as with evening sunshine. The second stone is white, and when it is stroked and dipped into clear water a medicine is dispensed which banishes all known disease. The third stone, green, gives its wearer victory in battle for he becomes the earth's most valiant warrior.

I should mention to your Majesty that the ring's charms would be wasted upon the lower creatures, such as chickens and rabbits. Their powers may be used only by animals of noble rank which is why, King of beasts, I set this ring aside as a gift for you alone.

Next to the amazing ring I came across a very singular comb and an extraordinary looking-glass. The comb was manufactured from the bone of a noble Indian panther, which is why it cannot be broken however unsuitably it is handled. Even its smell sends all misfortune packing. The teeth are polished like silver and between them it is possible to gaze into history and witness the wars of Troy, or catch a glimpse of the gods at play on Mount Olympus.

But let me move on to the mysteries of the looking-glass. With its help, one can see what is happening many miles away. I have learned, in fact, that King Solomon himself had it fixed to the roof of his famous temple at Jerusalem, where it prevented the growth of decay, dry rot, and other such nuisances. Now, the handle of the looking-glass is carved from the very same Lebanon cedar wood of which much of the Temple was built. And a further curiosity is that the world's greatest stories are written upon it in fine letters which, nevertheless, may very easily be read with the naked eye.

Perhaps your Majesties would care to hear the stories that are told on the looking-glass handle?

12 The Horse, the Ass and the Crane

The first story (went on Reynard) is about a wooden horse which a famous king made for his especially-beloved daughter. It was said that this remarkable beast could travel up to a hundred miles an hour, but the king's son, the prince, did not believe it. One day, being young and hot-headed, he jumped on its back, deciding to try it out for himself.

His father played a trick on him. When his son was not looking he turned a knob in the horse's side, and the animal promptly flew out of the palace window and soon reached a speed of ten miles a minute. No doubt the incident taught the rash young man a lesson.

The second story on the looking-glass handle is about another horse, only he was a real stallion that belonged to a farmer. One day it gave chase to a deer but hadn't much chance of catching it because the horse was too fat and slow. So he trotted up to a herdsman and said, "Catch that deer for me, and I will give you its flesh, skin and horns."

"How do you expect me to catch it?" demanded the herdsman. "I cannot run."

"I can," said the horse. "Jump on my back."

The herdsman obeyed and off they galloped at a fair pace. But, of course, the stupid horse had not stopped to think that if he couldn't run fast enough to catch the deer on his own, he was even less likely to do so with a man on his back. Too late he realized his mistake and neighed pitifully, "Get off, get off!"

"Not likely!" laughed the herdsman. "I have a whip, a bridle around your head and a pair of sharp spurs. You are my servant, now."

That is how the horse became a slave to man, which is quite as it should be. Perhaps the third story will please her Majesty, the Queen of beasts, for when we discover who stole the bundle containing the magic looking-glass it will be hers as a gift.

This time the characters are an ass, a dog and a rich farmer who owned them both. Not surprisingly, the farmer loved the dog the better, and when he was in the mood he made a great fuss of the animal, allowing him to lick his hands and face and share his company indoors.

Baldwin the Ass sometimes watched them through the window and thought, "Whatever can my master see in that useless dog? It never does a stroke of work whereas I toil from dawn till dusk, day in and day out. Yet there is that hound, eating with my master, sleeping on his best cushions, gobbling up bits of choice meat from the dinner table, but *I* have to live on nettles! Tomorrow I am going to earn myself some of that luxury and comfort."

So next day the Ass waited until the farmer came home through the gate, then galloped up to him, stood on his hind legs and placed his front hoofs affectionately on the man's shoulders. Then he licked the farmer's face with his big, rough tongue until the poor man's skin was red and painful. The farmer was simply terrified. Not able to make any sense of what was happening he yelled at the top of his voice, "Help, the Ass is trying to murder me!"

Along hurried the farmer's servants with their sticks, rakes and other weapons and beat the Ass mercilessly until it was glad enough to crawl back to its stable and nettle salad. It goes to show that asses and such creatures should not get ideas above their station in life.

Perhaps you are thinking that a wooden looking-glass handle could scarcely contain any more stories, but you would be quite wrong! The next tale, as it happens, concerns my own father and Tibert the Cat. Believe it or not, those two were at one time the best of friends. What spoiled it all was an incident which occurred the day they saw hunters galloping towards them across a certain meadow.

"Where shall we run?" asked my father, hearing the braying of hounds. "So long as we stick together we will be quite safe, because I know a thousand tricks for getting rid of hunters."

"Then good luck to you," cried Tibert the Cat. "I know only one trick – and here it is!"

And with that, the cowardly wretch leapt into a

tree and left my father to face the pack on his own. Of course, my father was so taken by surprise that he was not sure what to do.

"What about all those tricks you mentioned?" jeered the Cat.

My father was lucky to escape that day, and the tale shows what detestable animals all cats are, with their slippery, snide ways. Not, in my opinion, that wolves are any better. In fact, the looking-glass handle tells a story of one such fellow which will show you just what a sly creature he is.

One day this Wolf found a dead horse. Most of it had already been eaten so there were only a few bones left to pick over. It was not long before the Wolf, being too greedy, managed to get a bone stuck in his throat and he spent the rest of the day running here and there, howling with fright and misery, looking for a doctor kind enough to pull it out.

Quite by chance he met the Crane which, as is well known, is gifted with a long slender beak. "Good Crane," gurgled the Wolf. "Pull this bone from my throat and I will reward you well."

The Crane, being a kindly bird, reached into the Wolf's mouth and removed the bone in a twinkling.

When he had finished the Crane sat down patiently and waited for his reward.

"Reward?" laughed the Wolf. "But you have had your reward. You hurt me so much with your probings and pullings that you deserve to have your head

bitten off. The reward is that I am refraining from doing so. Now, be off with you and be grateful!"

Having got to the end of this story, Reynard the Fox sighed deeply and moaned, "Oh, alas! They were such wonderful gems. Who can have stolen them? Whoever did it deserves to be skinned alive. One of the reasons for sending them to your Majesties was that my own little cubs spent hours amusing themselves reading the stories on the looking-glass handle and watching the delightful pictures through the comb teeth, and I was afraid the gems would be mislaid. It is now perfectly clear that I made a mistake trusting that grass-eating Ram to deliver them."

Now even the Fox's worst enemies at court admired his talent as an actor, while those most easily charmed by his smooth tongue were thinking, "Can this Reynard be as much of a rogue as we thought?"

Reynard the Fox was well pleased with the effect of his tale-spinning on all of them, so he decided there could be no harm to his cause if he continued to amuse and instruct them.

That is why he told the story of the Wolf and his liver.

13 The Wolf and his Liver

Your Majesty seems very thoughtful (continued the Fox). Can it be that you are recalling the day my father cured *your* father, the late King of beasts, of a deadly sickness? But, of course, your Majesty was a very young lion cub at the time and you may have forgotten that my father was, in those days, a very famous and learned physician. He went around dressed, as was suitable to one of his high rank, in silken clothes girded by a belt of solid gold.

One day he arrived at the palace and learned that the King was so ill that he was not expected to live another hour. This distressed my father a great deal, for he was a loyal and loving subject, and he demanded to be allowed to treat the King himself.

Having been shown to his Majesty's bedchamber, my father took his pulse, examined him carefully, then gave his opinion: "Only one medicine will cure the King and that is the liver of a seven-year-old wolf."

As it happened the Wolf was standing by the bed at the time, and his Majesty turned wearily to him and said, "You hear what the doctor says, Sir Isegrim? Only your liver can save my life."

The Wolf turned pale. "Not *mine*, your Majesty – I am not yet *five* years old!"

"That is not important," said my father. "Let us take out his liver in any case – then I can tell whether it is of any use!"

So the Wolf was carried away, his liver removed, and as soon as the King had eaten it he was cured. His Majesty was very grateful, awarded my father a knighthood (after which he became known as Sir Fox) and presented him with a garland of roses which he wore around his neck.

But this is all forgotten these days, because the world has grown greedy and ungrateful, and those in power think only of lining their pockets! I well remember the time, O King of beasts, when three of us – yourself, Isegrim and I were out hunting together. Who was it that shared the carcasses, providing you with choice morsels to take home to our beloved Queen? And who grabbed all the juiciest pieces of meat for himself, leaving the rest of us only a few dry bones to gnaw? Why, I did the sharing and Isegrim did the snatching; and I mention this not out of conceit but because I am sworn to tell only the truth to this court. Why, I recall your very words to me after the hunt, your Majesty: "How kind and unselfish you are, dear Reynard. What a splendid example you are to that greedy creature the Wolf, who plunders and steals and has such disgraceful table manners!"

So, your Majesties, what more can I say on my behalf except that I have ever been a loyal and devoted subject?

Now Reynard looked so crestfallen that the King of beasts pardoned him again. The only condition was that he should find out what had happened to the wonderful gems and bring them to the palace at once.

Nobody said another word against Reynard. But

the only reason Isegrim the Wolf remained silent was that he was so furious that he couldn't open his mouth.

When he did succeed in unlocking his teeth he howled at the top of his voice, "Wait! You have not heard what happened when the Fox met my wife, the She-wolf."

So the court had to listen to another tale.

14 The Fox and the She-wolf

O King of beasts (howled the Wolf), how can the court be so taken in by the Fox's incredible lies? The fellow's words are like shadows floating around the borders of fairy land. Let me tell you how he treated my poor wife, one winter's day, while they happened to be travelling together across a wide lake.

"I will teach you how to catch fish in a very artful fashion," said Reynard.

"Thank you, kind Fox," replied the She-wolf who, to tell the truth, can be very stupid on occasions. "How exactly is it done?"

"With your tail," said the wretch. "Wait till we are in the middle of the lake. That is where the shoals of fish are most plentiful, and they will not expect us there."

So they waded some distance from the bank, then the Fox said, "Now, dangle your tail as deeply as you can in the water. Wait, and in a few minutes' time you will feel a heavy cluster of fish clinging to its tip. Then simply heave your supper back to the bank."

To my wife's atonishment, for she knew the Fox's greedy nature, he did not stay to share the promised

feast but swam on to the bank where he sat watching under a willow tree.

The She-wolf allowed her tail to droop in the water and presently a cold wind blew across the lake. The water froze hard, and there was my foolish wife's tail stuck fast in the ice! She couldn't tug it out no matter how hard she tried. Hearing her howls of alarm, I raced to the scene and tried to release her tail. Not listening to the taunts of the Fox, we heaved together, but before we could get her tail free, the villagers were roused and along they hurried with pitchforks. We were beaten most unkindly, and if it hadn't been dark we would never have made our escape. What was more, my wife never did catch any fish!

Oh, if there be any justice in this world let Reynard, that malicious and murderous Fox, be punished as he deserves.

Naturally, everybody present became very indignant when they heard this story, but Reynard said jeeringly, "The Wolf cannot prove a word of his story. I admit to having taught his wife to catch fish with her tail, but was it my fault that she left it dangling in the water too long so that it got frozen? It is slanderous to say that I stood on the bank, under a willow tree, and mocked them. While the Wolf was out on some spree of his own, there was I risking my own life trying to pull his fat wife out of the lake. When I last saw her, being chased by those villagers, there were enough fish hanging on her tail to provide twenty suppers."

"Liar!" screamed the She-wolf. "What an oily tongue the Fox has, and what a wonder it is that he doesn't slip on it! Your Majesties, let me tell you of another occasion on which he tricked me most cruelly."

Then she told the court the tale of the two buckets.

15 The Tale of the Two Buckets

One day I arrived at a well (said the She-wolf) which worked in the following fashion. Two buckets were attached to a single chain, so that while one bucket was at the bottom the other hung at the top, the chain running over a pulley in the middle.

Now, Reynard the Fox, who pretends to be so clever can, on occasion, be as stupid as any half-wit. That day he had jumped into one of the buckets and of course it had promptly dropped to the bottom of the well. There he was stuck, for there was no one to haul him out.

Now, since as everyone knows I have a kindly disposition and dislike seeing fellow creatures in distress, I was prepared to help in any way I could. To keep the Fox from fretting – and to tell the truth he was shrieking and wailing in a most cowardly way – I decided to amuse him with a little talk while I tried to think of a way to release him.

"Good day, Fox," I said. "I have been fishing in the lake, but alas it seems as empty as a drum."

"Oh, Madam, what a pity," replied the Fox. "But you are more fortunate than you know. You have

just heard me screaming with delight and merriment, for I have found down here enough fishes to feed us for a month. Why not join me and share the feast?"

"But how?" I asked.

"Nothing could be easier. You simply jump into that bucket you see beside you, and it will carry you swiftly but safely to the bottom."

You will realize, of course, that it was not until afterwards that I understood how the well worked. Being faint and impatient with hunger, I jumped into the bucket at once. Down and down it went, and I had not yet reached the bottom when, to my astonishment, I saw the Fox, who is a skinny sort of animal, pass me on his upward flight in the second pail!

As soon as he reached the top, Reynard hopped out and leaned over the wall, taunting me. As for fish, I never caught a glimpse of any. I was forced to stay down there the entire day, hungry and afraid. In due course, the villagers arrived and amused themselves by throwing stones and sticks down at me, and how I ever managed to scramble out and make my escape I will never know.

Not satisfied with this villainous treatment, the Fox met me some hours later and continued his jeering. "Dame Wolf," said he. "It is better that *you* were hit by the sticks and stones than me, because your plump body has more fat on it and you can hardly have felt a single blow. Be thankful that we met this morning and that I had the chance to teach you so much about wells and buckets."

"It is all nonsense, of course," complained the Fox when the She-wolf had finished. "Let me tell you what really happened. In any case, it was not the She-wolf I met but her husband, that traitorous rascal of a wolf."

Then Reynard began:

One day I came across the Wolf in the forest. He was lying down with that pale, weak look he wears on his face whenever he pretends to be starving, and wants someone to fetch his food for him. Still, I took pity on him and said that I would walk along with him and we would hunt together. Every inch of the journey was spent in my having to listen to the fellow whining in the most sickening fashion, until eventually we arrived at a curious hole covered over with brambles.

"Such a place must be teeming with fish, or rats, or something of the kind," said I. "Why don't you go down and explore?"

"Not for anything in the world!" moaned the Wolf. "It may be dangerous. *You* go, and I will wait by this tree."

As everyone knows, the Wolf will always let even his best friends face danger for him, as long as he saves his own skin. Then he goes running off with tales of his own bravery!

Well, I poked my head into the hole and

discovered myself in a long tunnel with a dim light glowing at the end. I pressed on, and after crawling a few dozen yards I was horrified to come face-to-face with the She-ape. She had eyes like hot coals, her mouth was full of needle-sharp teeth and her claws were like button hooks. What a frightening spectacle she was! And, what was even worse, she had her children with her. Each one was bigger than me and an uglier bunch I never want to meet.

Nevertheless, I decided it would be wise to hide my real feelings, so I said, "Bless you, Aunt Ape, and bless all your beautiful children. Surely they are fairer than princes – so dainty and gracious. As for you, as soon as I heard you were unwell I hurried here at once to offer my sympathy."

"Welcome, Nephew," she croaked. "How often I have heard the King of beasts himself say that he values your opinion in all matters. I myself have often thought how much I would like to hand my children over into your care, for they could not hope for a wiser nor better father."

"Not at all, Madam," I answered, bowing low to hide my face. "I do not deserve such esteem. But tell me, is that your excellent cooking I can smell?"

The She-ape gladly invited me to share their meal, and when I tell you that it included such delicacies as reindeer meat and partridges, you will understand why I stayed for some time. When I eventually returned above ground, the Wolf was groaning abominably.

"You have been feasting," he said. "What about my share?"

"My dear cousin, what is worrying you now?" I asked him. "Down you go, and if you treat my aunt the She-ape politely you will partake of the most delicious supper you have ever imagined. Don't forget to tell her of her matchless beauty, and be sure to say that her children remind you of cherubs."

Off went the Wolf, and I put my ear to the hole to hear better what would take place.

"Oh, what terrible goblins are your ape-children!" said the witless wolf. "They make my hair stand on end. Would it not be a great kindness simply to pop them in a sack and drown them, before they grow an inch taller?"

It would be useless to pretend that my aunt was pleased with this suggestion. In fact, she uttered a frightening scream and said, "Who cares what you think of us? Make yourself scarce before I scratch our your eyes!"

"But what about the food?" begged the idiot. "I can smell cooking."

"The smell of it is all you are going to get," cried the She-ape, and when the Wolf tried to snatch a cutlet of reindeer meat and make off with it, the entire Ape family went for him tooth and claw. Is it any wonder that *he* reappeared with only one ear, and his coat slashed to ribbons?

"What happened?" I asked him. "Didn't you

behave politely to my aunt the She-ape as I told you to?"

"Certainly not," said the Wolf. "I told her the plain truth."

"More fool you!" I retorted. "Don't you know that when the truth is unpleasant, *nobody* wants to listen to it?"

16 Reynard Fights a Duel

At the end of this story Isegrim the Wolf bared his teeth, took off his glove and cast it at Reynard's feet. "You have now accused me of treason, cowardice, stupidity, greed and deception," he howled. "I shall listen to no more. Fox, I hereby challenge you to a duel to the death."

Reynard the Fox felt weak, for he was no hero at heart, but for the moment there seemed no way of wriggling out of this new predicament.

The entire court waited in silence for his reply. Then the Fox, noticing how blunt and worn the Wolf's claws were after his escape from the angry villagers, made himself tall and said in a brave voice, "Wolf, I accept. I choose my nephew, Grimbard the Badger, as my second."

"I choose the Cat and the Bear for mine," said Isegrim.

Preparations for the duel were swiftly made and while they were going on the She-ape took Reynard aside and told him, "Reynard, my dear, the Wolf is angry and strong and you must take great care. Come I will help you."

The She-ape had Reynard's hairy coat shaved off

and his body well rubbed with oil. "Ah, now the Wolf will be no match for you. When the fight begins, simply keep your tail between your legs so it cannot be pulled. Twist and turn in the most slippery way you can, then you will win easily."

Even the King and Queen of beasts laughed aloud when Reynard entered the arena looking like a shorn lamb. Yet when the duel got under way it was easy to see how the She-ape's ruse worked to Reynard's advantage. The Wolf could not grasp his oily body and, to confuse his opponent even further, the Fox smacked him with his tail and kicked dust clouds into his face. He also maddened poor Isegrim with insults, calling him "crooked nose" and "glass eyes" and so on, until the Wolf, beating at the empty air, wasted most of his strength in fury.

However, the Wolf's greater power told in the end, and fixing the puny Fox to the ground by his arms Isegrim growled through his teeth, "Now, Fox, give in – nothing can save you!"

"I surrender!" shouted Reynard the Fox. "Dear Cousin, let me go free and I will be your servant for ever. Any good I find I will share with you half-and-half. Your enemies will be my enemies, and together we'll rule the world. With your great strength and my cunning, who could stand up against us? Surely it is foolish for us to tear each other to pieces, as we are closely related, and blood, they say, is thicker than water."

"Talk, always talk!" hissed the Wolf. "Liar and

cheat, now that I have you at my mercy, of course you bellow empty promises, but everyone knows they are worthless. Say your last prayers, false monk, before I finish you off."

But so full of anger and gloating was Isegrim that he forgot to hold the Fox securely. In a trice Reynard had twisted out of his grasp, giving his foe no chance to seize his oily body again. Then with countless bites and scratches the Fox tore into the Wolf until the poor wretch was utterly defeated and howling for mercy.

"Enough!" roared King Lion. "The duel is finished and I declare the Fox the winner. Let the Wolf's friends carry him off and mend him as best they can."

So Bruin the Bear and Tibert the Cat took Isegrim away to stitch his wounds and offer him what comfort they could. Meanwhile, the creatures of the forest crowded around Reynard with congratulations, wanting to pat his slippery back and shake his paws. Afterwards their Majesties held a great feast as a tribute to the Fox. Every animal and bird in the kingdom flocked to the banqueting hall, and no one cared who was right and who was wrong in the contest – only who was the victor! Then the King of beasts stood Reynard at his right hand and made the whole court kneel and swear to serve him, as slaves serve their masters.

And when it was all over, the hero of the hour crept away, back to his secret lair in the forest, where in due course he grew a thick new coat and amused his wife and cubs by describing everything that had taken place.